Leprechaun in Late Winter

Magic Tree House® Books

#1: DINOSAURS BEFORE DARK
#2: THE KNIGHT AT DAWN
#3: MUMMIES IN THE MORNING
#4: PIRATES PAST NOON
#5: NIGHT OF THE NINJAS
#6: AFTERNOON ON THE AMAZON
#7: SUNSET OF THE SABERTOOTH
#8: MIDNIGHT ON THE MOON
#9: DOLPHINS AT DAYBREAK
#10: GHOST TOWN AT SUNDOWN
#11: LIONS AT LUNCHTIME
#12: POLAR BEARS PAST BEDTIME
#13: VACATION UNDER THE VOLCANO
#14: DAY OF THE DRAGON KING
#15: VIKING SHIPS AT SUNRISE
#16: HOUR OF THE OLYMPICS
#17: TONIGHT ON THE *TITANIC*
#18: BUFFALO BEFORE BREAKFAST
#19: TIGERS AT TWILIGHT
#20: DINGOES AT DINNERTIME
#21: CIVIL WAR ON SUNDAY
#22: REVOLUTIONARY WAR
    ON WEDNESDAY
#23: TWISTER ON TUESDAY
#24: EARTHQUAKE IN THE
    EARLY MORNING
#25: STAGE FRIGHT ON A
    SUMMER NIGHT
#26: GOOD MORNING, GORILLAS
#27: THANKSGIVING ON THURSDAY
#28: HIGH TIDE IN HAWAII

Magic Tree House® Research Guides

DINOSAURS
KNIGHTS AND CASTLES
MUMMIES AND PYRAMIDS
PIRATES
RAIN FORESTS
SPACE
TITANIC
TWISTERS AND OTHER TERRIBLE STORMS
DOLPHINS AND SHARKS
ANCIENT GREECE AND THE OLYMPICS
AMERICAN REVOLUTION
SABERTOOTHS AND THE ICE AGE
PILGRIMS
ANCIENT ROME AND POMPEII
TSUNAMIS AND OTHER NATURAL DISASTERS
POLAR BEARS AND THE ARCTIC
SEA MONSTERS
PENGUINS AND ANTARCTICA
LEONARDO DA VINCI
GHOSTS
New! LEPRECHAUNS AND IRISH FOLKLORE

Merlin Missions

#29: CHRISTMAS IN CAMELOT
#30: HAUNTED CASTLE ON HALLOWS EVE
#31: SUMMER OF THE SEA SERPENT
#32: WINTER OF THE ICE WIZARD
#33: CARNIVAL AT CANDLELIGHT
#34: SEASON OF THE SANDSTORMS
#35: NIGHT OF THE NEW MAGICIANS
#36: BLIZZARD OF THE BLUE MOON
#37: DRAGON OF THE RED DAWN
#38: MONDAY WITH A MAD GENIUS
#39: DARK DAY IN THE DEEP SEA
#40: EVE OF THE EMPEROR PENGUIN
#41: MOONLIGHT ON THE MAGIC FLUTE
#42: A GOOD NIGHT FOR GHOSTS

MAGIC TREE HOUSE® #43
A MERLIN MISSION

Leprechaun in Late Winter

by Mary Pope Osborne

illustrated by Sal Murdocca

A STEPPING STONE BOOK™

Random House 🏠 New York

Text copyright © 2010 by Mary Pope Osborne
Illustrations copyright © 2010 by Sal Murdocca

Visit us on the Web!
www.magictreehouse.com
www.randomhouse.com/kids

Educators and librarians, for a variety of teaching tools, visit us at
www.randomhouse.com/teachers

Library of Congress Cataloging-in-Publication Data
Osborne, Mary Pope.
Leprechaun in late winter / by Mary Pope Osborne ; illustrated by Sal Murdocca — 1st ed.
p. cm. — (Magic tree house ; #43)
"A Merlin mission."
"A stepping stone book."
Summary: Jack and Annie travel back to nineteenth-century Ireland to inspire a young Augusta Gregory to share her love of Irish legends and folktales with the world.
ISBN 978-0-375-85650-1 (trade) — ISBN 978-0-375-95650-8 (lib. bdg.) — ISBN 978-0-375-89466-4 (e-book)
1. Time travel—Fiction. 2. Magic—Fiction. 3. Tree houses—Fiction.
4. Brothers and sisters—Fiction. 5. Gregory, Lady, 1852–1932—Fiction.
6. Ireland—History—19th century—Fiction.
I. Murdocca, Sal, ill. II. Title.
PZ7.O81167Le 2010 [Fic]—dc22 2009016591

Printed in the United States of America

10 9 8 7 6 5 4 3 2 1

For Lillian Grogan Osborne Reynolds

And with special thanks to Dan Ringuette

Dear Reader,

A few years ago I visited County Galway in Ireland. I traveled through seaside towns along the rocky coast and took a boat out to the lonely Aran Islands at the mouth of Galway Bay. I loved the lush green sheep meadows of the countryside, the smell of peat fires wafting through misty rain, the cozy pubs where we had gingerbread and strong tea. Ever since that visit, I've loved Irish music and literature—especially the folklore of leprechauns, fairies, and legendary Irish heroes and heroines.

So now I want to share Ireland with you. Get ready for a journey to the enchanted countryside of Galway, to a time a hundred and fifty years ago, when mysterious creatures still hid in the forests and hills. Be careful not to let them see you, or you might be turned into a skunk or a weasel! But don't be afraid—just have a great time with Jack and Annie.

CONTENTS

"They can grow small or grow large. They can take what shape they choose. . . . They go by us in a cloud of dust; they are as many as the blades of grass. They are everywhere."
—from *Visions and Beliefs in the West of Ireland* by Lady Gregory

Prologue

One summer day in Frog Creek, Pennsylvania, a mysterious tree house appeared in the woods. A brother and sister named Jack and Annie soon learned that the tree house was magic—it could take them to any time and any place in history. They also learned that the tree house belonged to Morgan le Fay, a magical librarian from the legendary realm of Camelot.

After Jack and Annie traveled on many adventures for Morgan, Merlin the magician began sending them on "Merlin Missions" in the tree house. With help from two young sorcerers named Teddy and Kathleen, Jack and Annie traveled to places both mythical and real to do Merlin's bidding.

On their most recent missions, Jack and Annie found four secrets of happiness to help Merlin when he was in trouble.

Now Merlin wants Jack and Annie to bring happiness to others—by helping four creative people give their special gifts to the world. They have already helped the first two; now they are ready to find the third. . . .

CHAPTER ONE

A Beautiful Word

It was a chilly afternoon in late winter. Annie was doing her homework on the computer in the living room. Jack sat on the couch and stared at a blank page in his small notebook. He heaved a sigh.

"What's wrong?" said Annie.

"I have to write a story for school," said Jack, "and I'm stuck."

"Well, you'd better get unstuck," said Annie. "Mom and Dad said we have to get our homework done before we go to the theater with them tonight."

"I know," said Jack. "But I can't think of anything to write about."

"Why don't you do what you love to do?" said Annie. "Go outside and write down some facts about what you see. Then turn them into a story."

"Hey, that's a good idea," said Jack. "Thanks." He jumped up and grabbed his coat from the hall closet. Then, taking his pencil and notebook with him, he headed outdoors.

The early March weather was sunny but cold and windy. Jack looked around. Then he wrote down some facts in his notebook:

old snow in yard
sun sparkling on sidewalk

Jack looked up again. Treetops swayed in the March winds. Jack started to write about them. But when he looked down at his notebook, he nearly dropped his pencil. On the page were two large, fancy letters:

T K

"Oh, man!" whispered Jack. He dashed back in the house and into the living room. "Annie! Look!" Jack held up his notebook. "Look at *this*!"

Annie stared at the page. "Old snow . . . sun sparkling . . . Nice. . . ."

"No, not that!" said Jack. "The letters!"

Annie looked at Jack like he was a little crazy. "Uh . . . what letters?" she said.

Jack looked back at the page. "They're gone!" he said. "A big, fancy T and K!"

"T and K?" said Annie.

"Yes! For Teddy and Kathleen!" said Jack. "The letters just appeared on the page when I was outside! They were there! Really!"

"I believe you," said Annie. She jumped up from the computer. "Let's go."

"Wait, I have to get my backpack from upstairs," said Jack.

"Forget it! Come on! The tree house must be waiting for us!" said Annie.

"Okay, okay," said Jack. He quickly shoved his

notebook and pencil into a pocket of his coat.

Annie grabbed her jacket. "Mom! Dad! We're going to take a little break from our homework!" she called.

"Okay, but make it short! We have to leave for the theater by seven!" their dad called from the kitchen.

"We will!" said Jack.

Jack and Annie headed outside. They ran over the melting snow in their front yard and up the sun-sparkling sidewalk. They charged across the street and into the Frog Creek woods. They hurried between the windblown trees until they came to the tallest oak.

High in the branches was the magic tree house. Their friends from Camelot, Teddy and Kathleen, were looking out the window.

"Hello!" called Kathleen.

"Hi!" shouted Annie, waving.

"Good trick with the magic letters!" Jack called.

"We thought you'd like that!" said Teddy. "I just learned how to do it!"

Annie grabbed the rope ladder and started up. Jack followed her. They climbed into the tree house and hugged the young enchanters.

"So what's up today?" asked Jack.

"Where does Merlin want us to go now?" asked Annie.

"Merlin wants you to go to Galway, Ireland," said Kathleen.

"Ireland? Cool!" said Annie.

"Morgan sent us to Ireland once before—to the ninth century," said Jack.

"Yes. Well, this time you will go to Ireland in the *nineteenth* century," said Teddy. "To 1862, to be exact. Your mission is to find an imaginative and creative girl named Augusta."

"Augusta doesn't know yet what her talents are," said Kathleen. "She lives in a time when it is not easy for girls to explore their creativity. Your mission will be to inspire her, so she can give her gifts to the world."

"What does that word mean exactly?" asked Annie. *"Inspire?"*

"'Tis a beautiful word," said Kathleen, her sea-blue eyes shining. "It means to breathe life into a person's heart, to make her feel joyful to be alive."

"That *is* beautiful," said Annie.

"You may need some magic to help you," said Teddy. From the corner of the tree house, he picked up the magic trumpet that had helped them on their last journey. "Only this time . . ."

Teddy handed the trumpet to Kathleen. She held the shiny brass instrument for a moment. Then she tossed it into the air. The trumpet spun like a whirlwind. There was a flash of blue light— and the trumpet was gone! In its place was a thin silver pipe with six holes.

"What's that?" breathed Jack.

"An Irish whistle," said Kathleen. She plucked the instrument from the air. "When you face great danger, one of you must play it. It will make magical music. And anything the other one sings will come true."

"But remember," said Teddy, "its magic will work only once."

"Right," said Annie.

"Thanks," said Jack. He took the Irish whistle from Kathleen and put it into his pocket. "And did Morgan send a research book to give us information?"

"Not this time," said Teddy. "Morgan wants you to draw upon your own experiences in life to help you on this journey."

"No problem," said Annie.

Jack wasn't sure about that. He liked having a book of facts to help them.

"So how do we find Augusta?" said Annie.

"It should be easy to find her," said Teddy. "When you land in the county of Galway, Ireland, just ask anyone for directions to the Big House."

"Hold on." Jack pulled out his notebook and wrote:

County of Galway, Ireland
Augusta
Big House

"Got it," said Jack. "But how do we get to Ireland in the first place if we don't have a research book?"

"Point to the notes you just made and make your wish," said Kathleen.

"And when you are ready to come home," said Teddy, "use the Pennsylvania book as you usually do."

"Got it," said Jack.

"Go now, and help Augusta," said Kathleen. "She needs you."

Jack pointed to the words *Galway, Ireland* in his notebook. "I wish we could go there!" he said.

"Bye!" Annie said to Teddy and Kathleen.

"Farewell!" said Kathleen.

"Good luck!" said Teddy.

The wind started to blow.

The tree house started to spin.

It spun faster and faster.

Then everything was still.

Absolutely still.

CHAPTER TWO

The Big House

A cold wind blew rain into the tree house. Jack shivered. He was wearing an old overcoat and ragged trousers. Annie wore a scarf, a shawl, and a long red wool dress. They both wore scuffed, worn boots.

"So where are we?" said Jack. He and Annie looked out the window.

The tree house had landed in a tree at the edge of a green meadow dotted with woolly white sheep. Next to the meadow was a narrow lane. It ran uphill between low stone walls. Through the drizzle, Jack could see mist-covered mountains in the distance and a flash of silver sea.

"It looks like a scene in a fairy tale," said Annie.

"Yeah, a fairy tale with bad weather," said Jack.

"I wonder where the Big House is," said Annie.

"I don't know, but I'd like to get inside it now," said Jack.

"Me too," said Annie, shivering. "Let's go."

Jack crammed his cold hands into the pockets of his torn coat. In one pocket, he felt his notebook and pencil. In the other, he felt the Irish whistle. "I've got the whistle," he said.

"Good," said Annie. She held her red skirt and started down the rope ladder. Jack climbed down after her.

Annie pulled her shawl tightly around her shoulders. Jack turned up the collar of his coat. As they tramped through the wet meadow, he felt cold water seeping through holes in his boots.

Jack and Annie climbed over a stone wall onto the muddy lane. A horse-drawn wagon was

rattling toward them down the hill. The wagon was filled with squealing pigs.

"Excuse me!" Annie called to the driver. "Can you tell us where the Big House is?"

An old man with a tired, rugged face pointed back up the hill.

"Thanks!" said Jack.

The large wooden wheels of the wagon rumbled past, splashing Jack and Annie with mud.

"Yuck!" said Annie.

"Now we're cold and wet and *dirty*," said Jack.

"Yeah, we're going to look great when we get to the Big House," said Annie.

"So what do we do when we get there?" asked Jack.

"When we find Augusta, maybe we tell her that Teddy and Kathleen sent us," said Annie, "like we told Louis Armstrong in New Orleans."

Just thinking about their adventure with Louis Armstrong made Jack smile. "I don't know if that will work," he said. "His world seemed so different from this world. There it was so noisy and busy. Here it feels lonely."

"Well, we won't know until we find Augusta," said Annie. "Let's go."

Jack and Annie lowered their heads. They plodded up the lane, sloshing in and out of giant puddles. When they reached the top of the hill, they stopped. The muddy lane wound down, past more sheep meadows and some cottages, past a long stable and several barns.

At the end of the lane was a large open gate that led onto the grounds of a white mansion. Gray smoke rose from the mansion's chimneys.

"The Big House!" said Annie.

"Maybe the people who live there will invite us inside to get warm and dry by a fire," said Jack.

Jack and Annie started down the lane. As they passed the sheep meadows, black-and-white dogs barked at them. When they walked by several boys hauling wet hay, the workers looked up and eyed them suspiciously.

Jack was relieved to get to the gate and head toward the Big House. When they reached the front door, Annie lifted the heavy knocker and let it drop.

A moment later, the door opened. A pale teenage girl looked out. "Who are you? Why are you here?"

"Uh . . . well . . . ," started Jack.

"Are you the ones the butler sent for?" the girl asked.

"The butler?" said Jack.

"Yes, we are!" said Annie.

"Then you should go round to the *back*!" the girl said. Before Jack or Annie could ask for Augusta, the girl slammed the door in their faces.

"Nice," said Jack.

"I hope *she* wasn't Augusta," said Annie.

"Why did you tell her 'yes'?" asked Jack.

"It's a way to get inside the Big House," said Annie. "Come on."

Jack and Annie tramped through the mud to the back of the mansion. They stopped at a door beneath a large smoking chimney. Annie knocked again.

This time a young red-haired girl in a cap and apron opened the door. "Yes?" she said.

"Is your name—" started Annie.

"Who is it, Molly?" someone called from inside.

Molly? So she's *not Augusta,* thought Jack.

"Who are you?" Molly asked them.

"We're the ones the butler sent for," said Annie.

"You?" said Molly. She looked doubtful. "Well, come in and see him then."

Jack and Annie stepped inside.

"He's in the kitchen," said Molly. She started down the hall.

Jack and Annie followed Molly to the doorway of a dimly lit kitchen. The kitchen smelled of fish and onions. Pots and pans hung from a long rack over a big wooden table. A stout older woman was bent over the table, rolling out dough.

"Cook, here are the ones the butler sent for," said Molly.

The cook looked up from her dough and squinted at Jack and Annie. "*You're* the ones he sent for?" she said.

"Uh, yes, ma'am, that's us," said Annie.

The cook turned toward the fireplace. Next to

the fire an ancient-looking man with white whiskers sat slumped in a chair, snoring. "Mr. O'Leary!"

The old man jerked and opened his eyes.

"The ones you sent for are here!" the cook shouted, as if the man were hard of hearing.

The groggy butler peered at Jack and Annie. "I sent for *you*?" he growled. "Not possible! I sent for a coach driver and a blacksmith."

"Really?" said Annie. "I guess there was a mistake. But maybe there are some other jobs we could do around here."

"Well, what are you good for?" asked the butler.

"What do you mean?" said Jack.

"Do you know how to sweep the inside of a chimney?" said the old man.

"Um . . . no," said Jack.

"Pluck a chicken?" the cook asked.

"No way," said Annie.

"What about rats?" the butler said.

"What about them?" asked Jack.

"They're all over the cellar," said the cook. "Can you catch 'em?"

"I—I don't think so," said Jack.

"Then you're no good to us here!" snorted the butler. "Be on your way!"

At that moment, Jack heard the back door open and shut. A girl about Jack's age stepped into the kitchen. She wore a red cape and carried two large, empty baskets. Her wet hair was parted neatly down the middle and pulled into a tight bun in the back.

"Ah!" said the cook. "Welcome back, Miss Augusta!"

CHAPTER THREE

Miss Augusta

Jack and Annie looked at each other. *Augusta!*

The girl put down her baskets and took off her wet cape.

"Did you deliver your cakes to the poor, Miss Augusta?" asked Molly.

"Yes, Molly," said Augusta. "I visited seven cottages today."

"Seven? In this weather? You're an angel, Miss Augusta!" said Molly. "Always so kind to the poor."

"It is my duty, Molly," the girl said, "to help those less fortunate than myself." Her gaze rested on Jack and Annie. "And who are *these* poor children?"

"They're looking for work, miss," said the cook. "But I'm afraid they're sorry creatures, not good for anything. I was just sending them away."

"Oh, surely we must not turn them out so quickly, Cook," said Augusta. "How tired and miserable they look."

Jack didn't think they looked *that* bad.

"We *are* tired and miserable," Annie said. Her voice sounded sad. Her shoulders sagged.

Oh, brother, Jack thought. Annie was really acting her part.

"My poor dears, you must both come into the parlor and rest a bit," said Augusta.

"We would like that," Annie said pitifully.

"Follow me," said Augusta.

"Miss Augusta, surely you're not taking those dirty children into the parlor!" said the cook.

"We must always be kind to the poor, Cook, no matter how dirty they are," said Augusta. "We should give them something to drink if they are thirsty, and something to eat if they are hungry."

"You are *too* kind, Miss Augusta," said Molly, shaking her head.

"Well, at least make them take off their filthy boots," said the cook.

Jack and Annie pulled off their boots and socks and set them by the door. Their feet were red and raw-looking.

Augusta took two peeled potatoes from a bowl and put them in her pocket. Then she picked up a lit candle from the hearth. "Come, let me take you to the parlor," she said to Jack and Annie.

"Thanks, Augusta," said Annie.

"Show some respect!" the cook called after Annie. "Call her '*Miss* Augusta'!"

"Sorry!" said Annie. "Thanks, *Miss* Augusta."

Jack rolled his eyes. Why should he call her 'miss'? Augusta didn't look like she was any older than he was!

Holding her flickering candle, Augusta led

Jack and Annie out of the kitchen. The wooden floor creaked as they walked barefoot through a narrow hallway.

How are we ever going to inspire this strange, serious girl? wondered Jack. *She acts as if she's already a grown-up and treats Annie and me like babies.*

"We'll sit in here, children," said Augusta. She directed Jack and Annie into a large room with heavy curtains and dark furniture. The pale teenage girl who'd answered the front door sat on a sofa, knitting. Another teenage girl knitted beside her. They scowled when they saw Jack and Annie.

"What are you doing, Augusta?" asked the pale girl. "Why are you bringing those two into the parlor?"

"I invited them to tea, Gertrude," said Augusta. She turned to Jack and Annie. "Pay no attention to my sisters," she said. "Please, sit down."

"Augusta, have you gone mad?" said Gertrude.

"You cannot invite these two ragamuffins to sit in here!"

"Mother will be furious," said Augusta's other sister. "They're filthy! They're not even wearing shoes!"

Jack looked down at his muddy clothes and cold red feet.

"Cook made them remove their muddy shoes in the kitchen, Eliza," Augusta said. "I only wish I had nice, dry shoes to give them. Sit down, children," she said to Jack and Annie again.

Jack and Annie slowly sat down.

"You're going to get into trouble, Augusta . . . ," said Gertrude.

"Mother will never approve," said Eliza. Both sisters shook their heads as they went back to their knitting.

Augusta ignored her sisters and walked to a silver teapot on a sideboard. "Would you like some hot tea, my poor dears?" she asked Jack and Annie.

"Yes, Miss Augusta," said Annie.

Jack nodded. Hot tea sounded good. He still felt chilled from the cold wind and rain. There was a fireplace in the dreary parlor, but no fire was lit. Everything in the room seemed dark and gloomy, except for a few books on a table.

As Augusta poured tea into fancy china cups, Jack leaned closer to get a look at the books. One was titled *The Plays of William Shakespeare.* Another was called *The Tales of King Arthur.* Jack smiled to himself. Seeing those book titles made him feel a little more comfortable.

Augusta carried cups of tea to Jack and Annie. Then she pulled the potatoes out of her pocket and gave one to each of them.

"Thank you, Miss Augusta," said Annie.

Jack took a sip of tea, but it was too bitter and hot to drink. He took a bite of his cold potato, but it was too hard to chew.

"So, Miss Augusta, what do you like to do around here?" Annie asked. "What inspires you?"

Augusta looked puzzled. "I do not know what you mean," she said.

"What about reading books?" said Jack. "Have you read those books?" He pointed to *The Tales of King Arthur* and *The Plays of William Shakespeare.*

"Those books belong to my brothers," said Augusta.

"The time has not come for Augusta to read such books," said her sister Gertrude.

"Not until she is older," said her sister Eliza.

"Why?" asked Jack.

"Mother says *The Tales of King Arthur* and the plays of Shakespeare are not for young ladies," said Augusta.

"Really?" said Jack.

"Yes. But I'm afraid I sometimes peek at my brothers' books," Augusta said to Jack and Annie in a low voice. "I love stories. I remember every story I read or hear."

"I love stories, too," said Annie. "And I love books."

The two older sisters smiled. "Keep striving, my dear," said Eliza. "Perhaps one day you will learn to read."

"I already know how to read," said Annie. "Jack and I read lots of books." She pointed to the books on the table. "In fact, we know tons about

King Arthur, and we go see plays by Shakespeare with our parents. And one time, we even acted in a play by Shakespeare—*A Midsummer Night's Dream.*"

"It was at our school," Jack broke in, before Annie could tell them that she and Jack had actually met Shakespeare himself!

"*A Midsummer Night's Dream?*" said Augusta. She looked surprised.

"Don't listen to them, Augusta," said Gertrude. "I doubt these children have ever been to school— much less acted in a play by William Shakespeare."

"I suspect you are quite right, Gertrude," someone said.

A tall woman was standing in the doorway of the parlor. She wore a long black velvet dress and stood very straight. There was an icy look on her face as she stared at Jack and Annie.

"Oh! Mother!" said Eliza.

CHAPTER FOUR

What Are You Good For?

"Hi there!" Annie said cheerfully.

Augusta's mother did not reply. She was staring at Jack's bare feet. Her expression made him sink down in his chair.

"Do not blame Eliza or me, Mother," said Gertrude. "These are Augusta's friends, not ours."

"I took pity on them, Mother," said Augusta. "They were wet and miserable."

Her mother finally smiled. "Yes, daughter, I imagine they were. It's very nice to have pity for the poor, but dirty children should not be sitting in our parlor."

"They were hungry, Mother," said Augusta.

"Yes, and I see you have given them food," said her mother. "So it is time to take them out of the house *now.*"

Jack and Annie stood up. Jack was happy to leave. He felt like Augusta and her mother were talking about stray dogs or cats.

But Augusta sat very still and just stared at her mother.

"Go on—get them out of here, Augusta," said Gertrude. "They are not clean! They might even have bugs in their hair."

The mere mention of bugs made Jack's scalp itch. He and Annie both scratched their heads.

"See!" said Gertrude.

"Augusta . . . ," her mother said in a stern voice.

"Oh, all right! All right!" said Augusta, standing up. "I was trying to be kind! Come with me, please," she said to Jack and Annie. "I'll lead you down the lane a bit, at least past the sheepdogs."

As Augusta started out of the room, her mother

stopped her and pinched her shoulders. "Carry yourself straight, daughter," she said.

Jack couldn't imagine how the girl could carry herself any straighter.

Augusta led Jack and Annie back down the dark hallway, through the fish-smelling kitchen, past the ancient butler sleeping by the fire and the three kitchen maids and the cook. Without a word, she grabbed her red cape and pulled it around her.

"Where are you going, Miss Augusta?" asked Molly.

"I have been ordered to send these poor children back out into the storm," Augusta said.

Jack and Annie forced their feet into their stiff, wet socks and boots. Augusta held the door for them, then followed them outside, slamming the door shut behind her.

Even though it was still rainy and windy, Jack felt much happier outside the Big House than inside it. He and Annie followed Augusta past the gates and out to the lane. Augusta walked stiffly, leading them like a mother duck.

"What are we going to do about her?" Annie whispered to Jack.

"I don't know," whispered Jack. "She doesn't seem very creative or imaginative to me."

"Well, we have to *inspire* her! Come on!" said Annie. She and Jack hurried to catch up with Augusta.

"Miss Augusta!" said Annie, walking alongside her. "Do you like to sing? Dance? Paint? Play a musical instrument? Anything creative like that?"

"No," said Augusta. She sounded angry. Jack figured she must be mad at her mother for kicking them out of the Big House.

"Well, what about nature?" said Annie.

"What about it?" asked Augusta.

"Walking in the woods?" said Annie. "Trees? Birds? Does anything like that inspire you?"

"Not anymore. I *was* close to nature once," Augusta said. "I used to roam the woods with my younger brothers. They said I was like a robin with the eye of a hawk. I knew where to find the caves of the otters. I knew where to find the nests of wild birds."

"That's so cool," said Annie.

"I knew where the deer lay down to sleep," said Augusta. "I knew the names of every tree: oak, beech, elm, hazel, larch, pine. . . ." Augusta's voice grew a little wobbly, as if she might cry. "But I'm not allowed to roam the woods with my brothers anymore. Mother says it's not proper for a young lady."

"That's so sad!" said Annie.

"Never mind," said Augusta, lifting her chin. "Let us not talk about me anymore. Let us try instead to help the two of you. Cook said you were not good for anything. Why would she say that?"

"They asked us if we were good for cleaning chimneys, plucking chickens, or catching rats," said Annie, "and we said no."

"Then you must find other ways to make yourselves useful," said Augusta, "or you will never find your way in the world. Can you shear sheep?"

"We've never tried it," said Jack.

"Milk cows? Churn butter? Weave a shawl?" Augusta asked impatiently. "Hunt rabbits with hounds?"

"Oh, never that!" said Annie. Jack laughed.

Augusta frowned. "This is nothing to laugh about. Every day, you must ask yourselves: what am I good for?"

Actually, that was a good question, Jack thought. What *was* he good for?

"And I would like to give you a further piece of advice," said Augusta. "Never make up stories about yourselves that aren't true."

"What do you mean?" said Jack.

"You never acted in a play of Shakespeare's, did you? Tell the truth now," said Augusta.

"We did," said Jack. "My sister *was* telling the truth. We were both in *A Midsummer Night's Dream*."

"We played wood fairies," said Annie. "We had green costumes, and Jack gave a little speech and I danced and sang."

Augusta shook her head. "You poor dears," she said. "I know you only make up these wild stories because your real lives are so miserable, but—"

"Wait a minute. Stop," said Jack. "What's wrong with you? Why do you act so snobby?"

"Snobby? *Me?*" Augusta looked confused.

"Jack—" said Annie.

"No, I'm serious," Jack said to Annie. "She thinks she's better than us."

"No, I don't!" Augusta said, stunned. "I'm not like that at all! Each day I walk several miles to town to give cakes and clothes to poor children like yourselves."

"That's nice," said Jack. "But you think you're better than those poor children, don't you? You'd never want to be real friends with them, would you?"

"What you say about me is *not* true!" Augusta said to Jack. "I love the poor! Why, my favorite friend in all the world is quite poor and has never been to school. Some say she's even a little cracked in the head, but I love her dearly!"

"Who's that?" asked Annie.

"Mary! Mary Sheridan, our old nursemaid," said Augusta. "I'll take you to meet her. Mary will tell you the truth about me! Come along!"

Augusta ran from the lane and across the muddy grass, her red cape flying in the wind.

"Um . . . I don't think you inspired her," Annie said.

"I know, I'm sorry," said Jack. "I just couldn't take her attitude any longer."

"Well, get over it," said Annie. "We're supposed to help her, not annoy her."

"She was annoying *me*!" said Jack.

"Yeah, I know," said Annie. "Me too. But we've got a mission. Come on."

Jack and Annie followed Augusta across the grass to a small white cottage with a straw roof. Augusta banged on the door, scaring away birds eating crumbs by the front steps. "Mary! Mary! It's me, Augusta!" she called.

"Come in, my dear," a voice answered.

Augusta lifted the latch and led Jack and Annie inside.

Wrapped in a brown shawl, Mary Sheridan was stroking an orange cat by an open fire. She had ragged white hair and bright blue eyes. Her crooked smile revealed a few missing teeth.

"One and twenty welcomes on this *wonderful* winter day!" said the old woman.

CHAPTER FIVE

A Fireside Tale

"Hello, Mary!" said Augusta. She kissed the old woman on her wrinkled cheek.

With the firelight on her face, Mary seemed to glow. Her warm, snug cottage was the opposite of the Big House. It smelled of damp leaves and moss, bread and chocolate. Firelight danced on the earthen floor and stone walls. Rain dripped through the roof, *pinging* into a couple of tin buckets.

"And who do we have here, Miss Augusta?" Mary asked.

"Two poor children from town," said Augusta. "I want you to tell them about me—how I truly love the poor and try to help them."

Mary smiled. "Please, sit down first," she said.

Jack, Annie, and Augusta sat down on three rickety wooden chairs.

"Would you children like some hot cocoa?" Mary asked.

Jack and Annie nodded eagerly.

"Yes, please, Mary," said Augusta. "But would you tell them—"

"Yes, I will tell them all about you," said Mary. She picked up a pot sitting on the hearth. She poured steaming cocoa into three mugs and handed them to Jack, Annie, and Augusta.

The cocoa smelled delicious. Jack took a sip and licked his lips. "Yum," he said. His insides felt warm for the first time all day.

"Now, Mary?" asked Augusta.

"In time, my child," Mary said to Augusta. "Tell me, what have you been doing today?"

"I delivered cakes in town," Augusta said proudly. "Then I found these poor children in our kitchen looking for work. I've tried to help them. But they say I am snobby. I brought them here so you could tell them the truth about me."

"Ah, I see, Miss Augusta. How did you try to help them?" said Mary.

"I've tried to discover what they are good for," said Augusta. "But it appears they are good for nothing."

"Really?" Mary fixed her twinkling eyes on Jack and Annie. "Well, let us start with this, children: tell me something you like to do. No, wait— what do you *love* to do?"

"Uh . . . well, I love to read," said Jack.

"And write," said Annie.

"Read and write?" said Augusta. "I don't think so."

Mary ignored Augusta and kept looking at Jack and Annie. "What do you like to read and write?" asked Mary.

"Facts mostly," said Jack. "True stories."

"Jack writes facts down all the time," said Annie.

"Honestly, Mary," said Augusta. "Soon they'll be telling you that they are actors, too—and have performed in a play by William Shakespeare. Can we talk about me now?"

"Actually, that's *true*," Jack said to Mary. "We were in *A Midsummer Night's Dream*. Annie and I were fairies. I had stage fright, but Will—"

"William Shakespeare *himself*," said Annie.

"He helped me get over it," said Jack. He looked straight at Augusta.

Augusta rolled her eyes.

"Will was *so* nice," said Annie.

"And smart," said Jack.

"Of course he was!" said Mary. "You can tell that from his stories."

"Oh, please stop. Don't tell Mary those ridiculous things!" Augusta said. "What about me, Mary?"

"Wait, child, I have a question for them," Mary said. She leaned forward and spoke in a whisper. "Where is summer? Can you answer me that?"

Mary's question doesn't make sense, Jack thought.

"I don't know. Do you know where summer is, Mary?" asked Annie.

"Summer is hiding with the Shee!" said Mary, laughing.

"The Shee? What's that?" said Annie.

"Surely, you must know the Shee," said Mary.

"That's what we Irish call our fairies. In the winter, the Shee steal all the warmth and sunshine, leaving us to suffer with the cold and rain!"

Annie laughed, too.

"So you've played the parts of fairies in a play by Shakespeare?" said Mary. "They're just like our Shee. Have you seen the Shee here in Ireland?"

"Mary!" Augusta said impatiently.

"Not yet," said Annie.

"That's a shame," said Mary. "I have seen them. This is a true story"—she looked at Jack and smiled—"with facts. You might want to write them down."

"Oh. Sure," said Jack. He pulled his notebook and pencil out of his pocket. Augusta looked surprised.

Mary leaned close to Jack and Annie again. Her eyes were shining and her voice was hushed. "One day long ago, a lonely young girl took a walk in an old forest," said Mary. "All was still, until joyful music began coming from a hidden world. . . ."

Jack loved Mary's way of telling a story. He wrote down:

old forest, all still
joyful music, hidden world

Augusta frowned. "So, I guess you *can* write," she muttered.

"Suddenly there came a spinning wind," said Mary, "and a cloud so bright, and a beam of light poured over a river!"

Jack quickly wrote:

spinning wind, bright cloud
beam of light, river

"Then they came, rumbling and thundering!" exclaimed Mary.

"Mary," said Augusta. She sounded impatient.

But Mary kept talking. "Some with wings, some on horses of white! Queens and kings! In robes and gowns the colors of summer, fall, winter, and spring!"

Jack wrote:

> some with wings
> white horses
> queens, kings

"They galloped in a circle, a blinding swirl!" said Mary. "They swept up that lonely girl and carried her across the river to their secret hollow hill! Had she gone inside, she would have become very small and seen many wondrous sights!"

Jack wrote:

> take lonely girl
> hollow hill of Shee
> wondrous sights

Jack looked up from his notebook, waiting for Mary to go on. When she spoke again, her voice was very soft. "But the girl grew afraid and ran home instead."

Mary sat back in her chair and closed her eyes.

The only sound in the cottage was the crackling of the fire and the *pinging* of rain into the tin buckets.

"Mary?" Annie said softly. "Are you the girl in the story?"

Mary opened her eyes. "I will never tell," she said.

"Oh, Mary," said Augusta, "such tales!" She turned to Jack and Annie. "Mary still believes in the impossible."

"Aye, I do, I surely do," said Mary. "Every night I leave a bit of milk on my windowsill for the Shee. I leave crumbs at my door. They eat them, too."

"Mary, the *birds* eat the crumbs!" said Augusta.

"Yes, the birds are hungry also," said Mary. "But the Shee pick over the crumbs first! At twilight, they steal across the river from their hidden hollow hills. Just ask the old fishermen of County Galway. Ask the farmers and nursemaids."

Augusta shook her head sadly. "Mary, only

simple-minded folk still believe in such things," she said. "Educated people know what is true and what is not true."

"No, child," said Mary. "They only know what they *think* is true. . . ."

Augusta straightened her shoulders. "Well. We should be going now, Mary," she said. "So could you please tell these children the truth about me now?"

"Yes," said Mary. She turned to Jack and Annie. "Do you children have names?"

Jack smiled. This was the first time today anyone had asked them their names.

"Yes. Our names are Jack and Annie," said Annie.

"Well, Jack and Annie, thank you for coming to visit me today. I can tell that you are very special," said Mary.

"What about *me*, Mary?" Augusta asked. "Am I special?"

"Yes, child, you are," said Mary. She turned to

Jack and Annie. "Augusta is special, too, but in a different way."

"How am I different, Mary?" asked Augusta.

"You try very, very hard to be good, and you are very smart. But you—" Mary stopped.

"What, Mary? I—what?" said Augusta.

"You are not happy," said Mary. "And that breaks my heart."

Augusta's eyes filled with tears.

"Oh, Augusta, don't cry," said Annie. She reached out to take Augusta's hand, but the girl stepped back.

Augusta wiped her eyes. "That's silly. I'm happy enough. I know I've never seen the Shee and I never will. But I don't care anymore. And if you like these miserable children more than me, Mary—well, that's fine!"

Augusta ran to the door and opened it. The damp air swept inside as she rushed out of the cottage. Through the open doorway, Jack and Annie could see Augusta's red cape flying behind her.

CHAPTER SIX

A Late-Winter's Daydream

Jack sighed. Their mission really seemed hopeless now.

"We'd better go find her," said Annie.

"She won't go far," said Mary. "My poor Augusta . . . she has a fine mind and a brave heart. But she is so unhappy."

"Why is she so unhappy, Mary?" asked Annie.

"Yeah, what is her problem?" said Jack.

"More than any of her brothers and sisters, Miss Augusta loved my stories," said Mary. "Remembered every one of them, she did."

"Really?" said Jack.

"Yes, she would repeat them back to me, word for word," said Mary.

"That's amazing," said Annie.

"She loved the stories so much that she grew desperate to see the Shee for herself," said Mary. "At night she would carry a lantern across the fields, calling for them. By day, she poked and prodded every part of the farm. Why, she even used a magnifying glass, scouring the earth for tiny footprints! But I'm afraid she never found them."

"Why?" said Annie.

Mary sighed. "Because she looked for them with her head and not her heart," she said. "Eventually she gave up and stopped searching. She didn't even want to hear the stories anymore. She's been a dutiful—but sorrowful—child ever since."

"That's terrible," said Annie. "What can we do to help her?"

"There is only one thing you can do," said Mary.

"What?" breathed Jack.

Mary leaned forward in her chair. Her blue eyes seemed to stare right through Jack and Annie. "You must show her the magic," she said.

What? thought Jack. *Does Mary know about the magic tree house?* "What do you mean?" he asked.

"I know that you children are like me—you see things that others don't," said Mary. "Help Augusta see them, too. Help her find the magic in the fields and in the forest."

For a moment, Jack and Annie didn't say anything. The wind blew through the open door. The fire crackled.

Then Annie took a deep breath. "Okay," she said. "We know exactly what to do."

"We do?" said Jack.

"Yep, we'll talk about it outside," said Annie. "Thanks, Mary. We'll find Augusta and take care of everything."

Jack and Annie stood up to go.

"One and twenty fare-thee-wells on this wonderful winter day," said Mary.

"One and twenty to you, too," said Jack. Then he and Annie left the cozy cottage, scattering the winter birds by the front door.

It had warmed up a little outside. The rain had stopped, but fog hung heavily over the sheep fields. The ground was soggy with mud.

Jack could barely make out Augusta's red cape through the fog. She was across the lane, sitting on a stone wall at the edge of the sheep meadow. "Mary was right, she didn't go far," Jack said. "So how do we show her the magic, Annie?"

"Easy," said Annie. "We play our magic whistle."

"No, we can't do that," said Jack. "We're supposed to save the whistle for a moment of great danger."

"That moment is *now!*" said Annie. "Come on."

"Hold on," said Jack. "What great danger are we facing right now?"

"Not us. *Augusta,*" said Annie. "She faces the great danger of losing all hope and happiness and being bored and sad for the rest of her life—and never being inspired and never sharing her gifts with the world! It's almost too late already!"

"Okay, okay," said Jack. "But are we just going to go up to her and start blowing the whistle and singing? That seems pretty weird."

"Hmm . . . yeah, it does," said Annie.

"How about this?" said Jack. "We'll tell Augusta that we want to put on a play for her."

"A play?" said Annie.

"Yep," said Jack. "We can tell her we want to prove that we weren't lying, that we really were in a play by Shakespeare."

"Oh, cool," said Annie. "Then what?"

"We play the magic whistle," said Jack. "We sing about the Shee. We make them appear— like in Mary's story—galloping and thundering! Augusta sees them. She gets inspired. Our mission's done."

"Perfect!" said Annie. "Let's go!"

Jack and Annie hurried across the lane to the

stone wall. "Excuse us, Miss Augusta," said Annie. "We just had a really great idea! Want to hear it?"

Augusta didn't answer. She kept staring at the ground.

"How would you like to see a play?" said Jack.

Augusta looked up. "A play?" she said.

"We want to put on our own play for you," said Annie.

"Why?" said Augusta.

"Because it's really good," said Jack. "And maybe it will prove to you that we really *were* in a play by Shakespeare."

Augusta looked doubtful.

"Come on, you'll love it," said Annie. "Do you know a quiet spot where no one can bother us?"

Augusta bit her lip and looked around. Then she stood up. "All right," she said. "The river near the old forest. I used to go there with my brothers."

"Great!" said Annie.

Annie and Jack followed Augusta through the rain-soaked, misty meadow. They walked past grazing sheep, then down a slope toward a wide, rushing river. The river separated the sheep's meadow from an old forest. Jack could barely see the trees through the ghostly fog.

Augusta stopped on a low ridge above the riverbank, near some large rocks. "Here," she said.

"Good, those rocks can be our stage," said Jack.

Jack and Annie climbed the pile of small boulders and stood on a large, flat rock.

"Okay," said Annie. "The name of this play is *A Late-Winter's Daydream.*"

Not bad, thought Jack.

"And this is what's going to happen," said Annie. "Jack will be the narrator. I'll play the Irish whistle. And Jack will sing a song that tells the story."

"What?" said Jack. "Excuse us a minute, Augusta." Jack turned to Annie. "Why *me* sing?" he whispered. "Why not *I* play and *you* sing?"

"No, I want to play," said Annie. "You took notes at Mary's, right? So just say a few words to describe the scene. Then use your notes about the Shee to make up a song. You can do that, can't you?"

"I guess . . . ," said Jack.

"Cool," said Annie. "Give me the whistle."

Jack reached into his pockets and pulled out his notebook and the Irish whistle. He gave the whistle to Annie.

"Sorry, Miss Augusta," said Annie. "We're almost ready." She whispered directions to Jack. "Okay. Say your introduction. I'll start to play. Then you'll start to sing. Then—"

"I've got it," said Jack. "Let's just start."

Jack and Annie turned to face Augusta. Jack cleared his throat. Then he spoke in a loud voice:

All is still in an old forest—
until music sounds from a hidden world. . . .

Jack nodded to Annie.

Annie raised the magic Irish whistle to her lips and began to play.

Strange, sweet music came from the whistle. The music was both sad *and* happy. It was full of beauty and hope, pain and sorrow. Like the fog over the river, the music seemed to blend everything together.

For a moment, the whistle music was so powerful that Jack couldn't sing. He felt like crying and laughing at the same time. Finally he looked down at his notes and began to sing:

In the spinning of light—
in a cloud, like a dream,
a bridge appeared over
a wide, flowing stream.

Jack surprised himself. He thought his words for the song sounded pretty good.

A long, fluttering high note burst from Annie's whistle. Bright, dancing light flowed across the river. The light arched through the fog toward Jack, Annie, and Augusta.

Augusta gasped. Jack looked back down at his notes and sang:

Some came on horses,
some came with wings.
From an enchanted world
little queens, little kings!

The wind began to blow. Jack looked up. Leaves and grass and twigs were flying everywhere.

The whistle music grew wilder.

Thundering and rumbling sounds came from the old forest. A herd of very small white horses galloped out of the mist. On their backs were proud and lovely riders—men in gold helmets, women with long hair floating on the wind. Their capes and gowns were the colors of nature—the pale rose of a spring dawn, the green of summer hummingbirds, the blue of winter twilight, and the gold of autumn oak leaves.

"The Shee!" cried Augusta.

CHAPTER SEVEN

Willy

Hundreds of Shee swarmed over the bright bridge. Behind the galloping riders more Shee came fluttering on wings like butterflies.

Augusta stood up as if in a trance, her hands clasped over her heart.

"Oh, wow!" breathed Annie.

"Keep playing!" shouted Jack.

Annie blew into the whistle again.

The Shee flew and galloped along the wide, grassy bank. Their horses, fleet as the wind, had arched necks and flaming eyes. They moved faster and faster, swirling into a blinding circle of light and color.

The soaring sounds of the music inspired Jack to soar with his words, too. He looked at his notebook and sang:

> *In a swirl they leave,*
> *so wild, so free,*
> *with a lonely girl*
> *to the hill of the Shee!*

"Jack, no!" shouted Annie.

A mighty blast of wind nearly blew Jack and Annie off their rock. They crouched down and covered their heads. When the wind grew calm, they stood up—just in time to see the swirling cloud of light vanish back into the old forest.

The Shee were gone. Once again, sky blended with water and earth in a veil of silver mist.

"Whew," Jack said breathlessly. "That was amazing!"

"Jack! Do you know what you just did?"

"Yeah, I made the Shee appear and disappear," Jack said. "I used my notes from Mary's story, just like we planned."

"Yes, you did that," said Annie. "And you made *Augusta* disappear, too!"

"What?" said Jack.

"The Shee took Augusta!" said Annie. "I tried to stop you, but it was too late! You'd already sung those words—"

"What words?" said Jack.

"You sang: *In a swirl they leave, so wild, so free, with a lonely girl to the hill of the Shee!*" said Annie.

"I was just reading from my notes!" said Jack. "They took Augusta? Are you sure?"

"Yes! She's gone!" said Annie.

"Oh, no!" said Jack. He and Annie ran to the ridge above the river. "Augusta!" he shouted.

There was no sign of Augusta's red cape anywhere.

"See? She's gone," said Annie.

"It's all my fault!" said Jack.

"You couldn't help yourself," said Annie.

"But I'm responsible!" said Jack. "We have to get her back!"

"Maybe Mary can help us," said Annie. "She—"

"Wait, listen," said Jack. "What's that sound?"

Squeaky noises were coming from behind the pile of small boulders. It sounded as if someone was trying to play the magic whistle. But the sound was definitely not magical.

"The whistle! I must've dropped it!" said Annie.

"Maybe it's Augusta!" said Jack.

Jack and Annie ran back and looked over the rocks.

A man no higher than Jack's knee was blowing into the whistle. The man wore a green jacket and a three-cornered red cap with a white feather. He had big ears, a bushy red beard, skinny little legs, and silver buckles on his shoes.

"Oh, man," said Jack.

"A leprechaun!" whispered Annie.

Jack and Annie just stared at the leprechaun as he blew into the whistle. His small, bony fingers danced over its six holes. But only squeaks, chirps, and hollow tweeting sounds came out.

The leprechaun blew harder and harder. Then he stopped. He turned the whistle over and looked at it closely. He shook his head and frowned.

"Hello!" said Annie.

The leprechaun jumped and looked up. "Well, hello yourself!" he said, grinning. "You startled me! Here, take this back. It's no use to me, as you can plainly hear."

The little man held up the whistle. Jack reached over the rock and took it. He slipped it back into the pocket of his coat.

"Listen, we need your help," said Jack. "Our friend—"

"Oh, you humans! Always in such a hurry!" the leprechaun said.

"Sorry," said Jack, "but we really need you to help us. You see—"

"First of all, who are you?" the leprechaun asked.

"I'm Jack. She's my sister, Annie," said Jack. "Our friend—"

"Ah, well then, Jack and sister Annie, I'm Willy," said the leprechaun. "Now, let's get a few things straight right away—never call me Little Willy or Tiny Willy. I don't like it. And never, *ever* call me Wee Willy. That's the one I hate the most."

"Okay, fine!" said Jack. "But—"

"Jack, let me handle this," said Annie. She turned to the leprechaun. "Willy, why didn't you go back over the river with the Shee?"

"Ask me why I came over the river in the first place, and I'll tell you the answers to both questions," said Willy.

"Okay, why did you come over the river in the first place, Willy? *And* why didn't you go back across with the Shee?" said Annie.

"Answer number one: I was having a bit of a nap in the reeds when I heard your whistle playing," said Willy. "Before I knew it, I was moving with the Shee across the bridge. Probably you didn't see me. Lost in the swirl of things, I was."

"Excuse me—" started Jack.

"I've heard some good whistle playing," Willy said. "But yours, missy, was like none I've ever heard from a human—not in the nine hundred years of my life. So! Answer number two: I didn't go *back* over the river because I wanted to find out the secret of your playing. Well?"

"That's easy," said Annie. "The whistle played itself. It wasn't me."

"Ah, you're a modest girl," said Willy. "And you like to keep the secrets of your talents to yourself."

"Not really—" said Annie.

"Listen, Willy!" Jack broke in. "Can you help us? We lost our friend, Augusta. It was my fault. I sang about a lonely girl. Then she was taken by the Shee—"

"Yes, I saw that," said Willy. "Whisked away, she was. So I'm guessing now you want me to help you find her. Is that it?"

"Yes! That's it!" said Jack.

"We were going to ask Mary Sheridan to help us," said Annie. "But you probably know the way better. And—"

"Wait a minute," said Willy. "Did you say Mary Sheridan?"

"You know Mary?" said Annie.

"Know her?" said Willy, grinning from ear to ear. "Why, if I were four feet taller, I'd have married Mary Sheridan years ago."

"Really?" said Annie.

"Oh, yes, indeed, we're very good friends," said Willy. "You see, I live in what you might call the *In-between*. I have one foot in the magical world of the Shee. And I have one foot in the mortal world of humans, like Mary. Ah, lovely Mary . . ."

"Yeah, Mary's great," said Jack. "But now—"

"You want me to guide you to your missing friend," said Willy.

"Right, right!" said Jack.

"I can do that, but what will you give me for it?" said Willy.

"What do you mean?" asked Jack.

"What will you give me for helping you find your friend? My time's very valuable, you know," said Willy.

"We don't really have anything," said Jack.

"We're poor and miserable," said Annie.

"I can see that," said Willy. "All right then, how about this: I'll lead you to your friend, and you'll teach me how to play the whistle the way you play it. Fair enough?"

"Sorry, I—" said Annie.

"Deal!" Jack broke in.

"Jack?" said Annie.

"Annie, it's a deal," Jack said. He was ready to promise anything to save Augusta!

"Good!" said Willy. "I'd love to play like that for Mary someday. Now, the path I'm about to show you is very, very secret. You must never show another living soul."

"Of course not," said Jack.

"Then come with me," said Willy, "and I'll lead you across the water to the home of the Shee!"

CHAPTER EIGHT

The Hollow Hill

The leprechaun scrambled down the steep bank of the river.

Jack started to follow, but Annie grabbed him. "Jack, the whistle won't work for Willy!" she said.

"I know," said Jack. "We'll worry about that later. Right now, we just have to save Augusta! Come on!"

Jack and Annie hurried after Willy to the wide, rushing river.

"How do we get across?" Jack asked.

"Follow me along the river," said Willy, "and I'll show you. Step lightly."

Willy skipped ahead of them along the riverbank. Jack and Annie followed. Jack tried to step
lightly, but it was impossible. Slopping through the
mud, his boots filled with ooze and made squishing
sounds with every step.

The river grew narrower and narrower, twist-
ing and turning like a snake. The mist grew
thicker, until Jack could hardly see a thing. He
bumped into Willy, almost knocking him over.

"Careful, laddie!" said the leprechaun.

"Sorry," said Jack.

"All right," said Willy. "Here's where we cross.
Hop from stone to stone after me." Willy disap-
peared into the mist, crossing the river. Annie followed him.

Jack started across, too. He tried to hop care-
fully from stone to stone, but the stones were slip-
pery. On his third hop, his boot slid off a mossy
rock, and he splashed into the freezing water!

"Jack, are you okay?" Annie called in a loud
whisper.

"Yeah, yeah, I'm fine!" Jack said. He scrambled

up. His clothes were soaked and heavy. He really was miserable now. He waded to the other side of the river and joined Annie and Willy.

"Ah, you fell in," said Willy. "That happens sometimes. Come with me now, into the forest."

Jack, Annie, and Willy walked under the trees. They passed old oaks and maples that creaked in the wind. Jack shivered in his soaking wet clothes.

A big black crow called from a high, bare branch.

Willy jumped, then laughed. "Ah, 'tis probably Patrick Daly," he said. "Rumor is the Shee changed him into a crow for stealing a pair of the High Queen's shoes."

"Changed him into a crow?" said Jack.

Willy nodded. "One of the Shee's favorite tricks," he said, "changing humans who displease them into animals."

"Oh," said Jack.

A white rabbit scampered through the forest. "That bunny over there is no doubt the former

Mrs. Shan McCartie. She was rude to the High King," said Willy.

"Rude to the High King?" said Jack. He was starting to feel like he was trapped in a nightmare.

"The Shee cannot bear the rudeness of humans," said Willy. "Look there." He pointed to a fawn peeking out from behind a fir tree.

"Aww, it's so cute," said Annie.

"Cute? Maybe. Maybe not," said Willy. "Could easily be old John Foley. I heard he was changed just for being a grouch! Come along."

Willy led Jack and Annie through the forest until they came to a tangle of briars and brambles. "The hollow hill of the Shee lies just beyond this thicket," he said to them. "Do you still want to go and find your friend?"

"Yes," Jack and Annie both whispered.

"Then off you go, and good luck to you," said Willy, tipping his hat.

"What? Aren't you coming with us?" said Jack.

"Oh, my, no," said Willy. "The Shee would be

furious if they knew I'd shown humans the path to their secret hiding place. And I certainly don't want to live the rest of my life as a weasel."

"But won't they be angry at *us* for finding their secret hiding place?" said Jack.

"Possibly," said Willy. "Here's what I recommend you do: politely tell the High King and the High Queen that you've just come looking for your dear friend to take her back to her loving family. The Shee place very great value on friendship and family."

"Okay," said Jack. "Friendship and family . . ."

"And remember: be simple, direct, and honest at all times," said Willy.

"Simple, direct, honest," repeated Jack.

"And polite, that's the most important—very, very polite," said Willy.

"Very polite," said Annie. "Got it."

"Another thing," said Willy. "In the world of the Shee, the old tales still live. So do not be afraid if you see odd sights floating about. They're just bits and pieces of the old stories. Now go. Be simple, direct, honest, and polite, and save your dear friend before she's lost forever."

"Thanks, Willy," said Annie.

"Best of luck," said Willy.

"See you later," said Jack.

"Aye, I'll be waiting for you," said the leprechaun.

Jack and Annie crouched down and started through the thicket. Thorns and briars pulled at Jack's wet coat. They scratched his hands and got caught in his hair.

Jack battled his way through the tangled brush until he caught up with Annie. They both pushed their way out of the thicket and stepped into a glade.

"Wow, it's like Mary said," whispered Annie. "It *is* like summer here."

No rain fell. No wind blew. Warm sunshine shone on the emerald-green glade. In the middle of the glade was a large grassy mound. At the foot of the mound was a small doorway framed by stones.

"That must be it—the hollow hill," said Jack, "the secret home of the Shee."

"And *that* must be someone from an old story," whispered Annie. She pointed to a woman floating above the green mound.

The woman wore a wreath of flowers on her head and carried a branch with silver apples. She vanished in the sunny haze.

"Whoa," whispered Jack.

A small sailing ship then appeared in the air. It had white sails and flags flying. The ship, too, vanished. Then an old woman spinning at a spinning wheel appeared . . . then a wispy dragon . . . then a knight with a sword. The parade of images faded into the sunshine like wisps of smoke.

"Whew," said Jack.

"Listen," said Annie.

The sound of drumming was coming from the doorway of the grassy mound. "Come on, let's look inside," said Annie.

Jack and Annie snuck close to the small

doorway. It was no higher than Jack's waist. He and Annie knelt down and peeked inside.

The hollow hill was filled with a pale-green light. Very small dancers, none more than eight inches tall, were bathed in the light. As drummers pounded tiny drums, the dancers danced together in rows. They held their arms straight by their sides and kicked their legs and turned around and around to the rhythm of the drums.

A small shining couple sat on high golden chairs watching the dancers. They wore golden crowns.

"They must be the High King and the High Queen," whispered Annie.

Jack and Annie watched until the rows of dancers parted. Then they could see a third person watching the dance. She was no taller than the dancers. Draped around her shoulders was a red cape.

"It's Augusta!" said Annie.

CHAPTER NINE

Skunks or Weasels?

"Augusta!" whispered Jack. "She's—she's tiny!"

"They must have shrunk her!" whispered Annie.

"Hide!" whispered Jack. He crawled away from the door. Annie crawled after him. They pressed their backs against the grassy mound.

"Why are we hiding?" asked Annie.

"We can't let them see us!" said Jack. "They might shrink us, too!"

"But how are we going to save Augusta?" asked Annie.

"I don't know," said Jack.

"Hey, I just remembered something," said Annie. "Didn't Mary say the girl in her story would have become small *if she'd gone inside the hollow hill*?"

"Yeah, she did," said Jack. "So maybe that means you can only get shrunk if you go inside."

"Right," said Annie. "So let's go back to the doorway and call from outside. We'll be simple, direct, honest, and very polite, like Willy said. We'll tell the king and queen we've come to take our friend back to her family."

"But wait a minute," said Jack. "How can she go back to normal life with her family if she's only eight inches tall?"

"Good point," said Annie.

"This is so weird," said Jack.

"Let's worry about her size later," said Annie. "For now, we just have to help her escape."

"Right," said Jack. "Let's try it."

Jack and Annie crawled back to the entrance

of the hollow hill and peeked inside.

In the pale-green light, a very small Augusta stood watching the dancers.

"Excuse us, please!" Annie called.

The drumming stopped. The dancers froze. All eyes turned to Jack and Annie. The High King and High Queen looked startled.

"Who are you?" the king called. "How did you find us?"

"That's not important!" said Annie. "We are *very* sorry to bother you! But we've come to get our *very* dear friend Augusta! We have to take her home to her *very* loving family!"

"Please! Thank you!" added Jack, trying to sound polite.

Before the king or queen could speak, Augusta rushed forward. "No! I don't want to go home!" she screamed in a high little voice. "I don't want to leave the Shee!"

"Whoa," said Jack. That was a surprise. Maybe Augusta was under a spell!

"Leave here at once!" the High King commanded Jack and Annie in a squeaky voice. "You were not invited! You have no business here!"

"Yes, we are leaving right away. But Augusta has to come with us!" Annie called. "Thank you!"

"She's right!" said Jack. "Augusta has to come with us, please. Thank you!"

"No! I want to stay here!" said Augusta. "I'm not good for anything at home! Mary was right, I'm not happy there!"

Jack was amazed—Augusta *wasn't* under a spell. She really wanted to stay with the Shee!

"The girl will stay with us!" the High King shouted. "Go, now! *Now!*"

"No way!" Jack blurted out. "We won't leave without Augusta!"

The crowd gasped.

"What?" roared the High King.

"Sorry, sorry," said Jack. "I meant—"

"You will pay for this rudeness!" the king yelled.

Before Jack and Annie could get away, the king thrust out his arm. Sparks flew from the tips of his tiny fingers. Suddenly Jack and Annie couldn't move their arms or legs!

The king kept pointing at them. "Skunks?" he shouted at the crowd. "Or weasels?"

"Neither, please! Thank you!" shouted Jack. He was glad he could still talk!

But the crowd began chanting in strange, high voices, "Skunks! Skunks! Skunks!"

The king nodded and raised both arms into the air. Jack was desperate. He didn't want to live the rest of his life as a skunk!

"Wait! Please!" Jack shouted. "I'm sorry I was rude! Before you change us, I really, really need to tell Augusta some things! Thank you!"

The king looked at Jack for a long moment. Then he lowered his arms, and the crowd grew silent.

"Thank you!" said Jack. "Augusta, listen to me! You should go back home. You're good for lots of things back there! You're very kind! And Mary said you have a brave heart and a fine mind! Those are really good things to have!"

Tears rolled down Augusta's cheeks. She shook her head.

"Listen to me, please!" Jack went on. "Mary

says you're not happy. But some things do make you happy, Augusta. You said you feel close to nature! You said you love simple folk like Mary. And I know you love stories, too! Mary said you remembered every story she told you! You used to tell them yourself, word for word! You have a great memory!"

"He's right, Augusta!" yelled Annie. "Those are your gifts! You need to give your gifts to the world!"

Augusta was still for a moment. Then she shook her head. "I want to stay!" she said.

"You have had your say!" the High King shouted at Jack and Annie. "Now prepare to become skunks!" He raised his arms again.

Oh, no! thought Jack.

"Wait, Finvara!" said the High Queen.

The High Queen stepped closer to Augusta. The queen wore a silver cloak that glittered with diamonds. She had jewels in her long red hair that shone like stars. Her high, clear voice rang like a bell. "I am Queen Aine of the Shee," she said. "The boy said you love stories—and that you remember every story you hear. Is this true?"

Augusta nodded.

"Then listen now to *our* story," said Queen Aine.

All the Shee were very still, watching Augusta and their queen.

"In the morning of time, out of a rosy sky and a windy light, we came," said Queen Aine. "We were tribes of a supernatural people called the Tuatha Dé Danann. Strong, fearless, and noble we were. Five roads carried our armies through the wild, wooded lands of Ireland, and for eons we ruled the Irish world.

"But when the humans came, the wild woods gave way to villages and pastures. Our tribes hid in the hollow hills, in ruined forts, and under the sea. Over time we made ourselves smaller and smaller so we could more easily hide from humans.

"Eventually we became known as the Shee, and we were mocked as the Wee Folk of Faerie. But, in truth, we are a tribe of the great Tuatha Dé

Danann, and we live in enchanted places like this one, protected by what is left of our magic. Do you understand?"

"I do, yes," breathed Augusta.

"Our stories were passed down for centuries in the old language of Ireland. But as the old language was replaced with English, the stories began to fade away," Queen Aine said.

"Go home now with your friends, human child. Go back, for our sake. Seek out the old storytellers, and ask them to tell you the tales of my people. Learn the old language. Read the old manuscripts. Write our stories down and share them before they are lost completely. Share them with all the people of Ireland and all the world. Will you do that for us? Will you use your gifts to tell our stories and restore our dignity?"

Augusta's eyes shone. "Yes," she said, "yes, I will, yes."

"Good. Then I will send you all swiftly home," said Queen Aine. She beckoned to a small dancer, who stepped forward with a tiny silver chalice.

"Sip the honey nectar of the Shee," said the High Queen. She took the chalice and held it out to Augusta. Augusta took a sip.

A second later, Jack felt cold wind and rain. He and Annie were standing on the bank of the river. Augusta was standing beside them. She was her normal size again.

CHAPTER TEN

Fare-thee-wells

"**W**ell, *that* was simple and direct," said Annie.

"Yeah. . . ." Jack felt dazed.

Augusta looked at Jack and Annie. "I saw them," she said, her eyes wide. "I finally saw the Shee. I really saw them!" She burst out laughing. Her laughter was so full of joy that Jack and Annie started laughing, too.

"I saw them! I saw them!" Augusta kept repeating. "I saw the Shee! And now I have important things to do!"

"Yes, you do," said Annie.

"I must learn the old language! And I must start gathering stories at once, that's what Queen Aine told me!" said Augusta. "I can't wait to visit the old storytellers! There's Mary Sheridan and Biddy Early, too! I'll start with Mary! Let's go see her right now! Hurry! Will you come with me? Hurry!"

"Sure," said Annie, "but just a second." She turned to Jack. "What about Willy?"

"Who's Willy?" asked Augusta.

"A friend of ours," said Jack, looking around. "He said he'd wait for us. But where was he going to wait? Willy!"

"Willy!" called Annie.

"I guess he's still somewhere on the other side of the river . . . ," said Jack.

"That's too bad," said Annie.

"Yeah," said Jack.

"Come, let us go see Mary now!" said Augusta, grabbing Annie's hand and pulling her along.

Jack looked around for Willy one last time. He

was sad about not seeing the leprechaun again. But he was a little relieved, too. He knew they couldn't keep their part of the deal: teaching Willy how to play the magic whistle.

"Come on, Jack!" cried Augusta.

Jack followed the two girls through the wet meadow, over the stone wall, down the dirt lane, and across the muddy field to Mary Sheridan's cottage.

"Mary! Mary!" Augusta called. She dashed ahead of Jack and Annie. She didn't even stop to knock. She threw open the door to the cottage. "Oh!" she said, freezing in her tracks.

Jack and Annie caught up with Augusta and looked inside.

Mary was sitting in front of her fire. Next to her was a small man wearing a green jacket and a three-cornered red cap with a white feather.

"Willy!" cried Annie.

Annie and Jack hurried past Augusta into the cottage.

"You're here!" said Jack.

"Of course! I said I'd wait for you!" said the leprechaun. "I see you found your dear friend and brought her home. Good work!"

Augusta stood in the doorway, gaping at Willy. "Who are *you*?" she asked.

"Name's Willy. Just plain Willy," said the leprechaun. "I usually leave before you visit Mary. But now that you've seen the Shee, I suppose there's no point hiding from you anymore."

"Are—are you real?" asked Augusta.

"Who knows?" said the leprechaun. "Maybe *I'm* real and you're *not*! Depends on which one of us is asking the question!"

Everyone laughed. "Good point," said Annie.

"Well, we'd better be getting home," said Jack. He wanted to leave before Willy asked Annie for his whistle lesson.

Jack took Annie's hand and started backing toward the door. "Thanks for helping us, Willy," he said.

"Yeah, and thanks, Mary, for everything!" said Annie, waving. "Good-bye, Augusta! Good-bye, everyone!"

"Wait just a minute, my friends," said Willy.

Uh-oh, thought Jack.

"Have you forgotten our deal?" said Willy. "My fingers are itching to make beautiful music for Mary."

"Well, you see . . . there's a problem with that," said Jack, squirming.

A frown crossed Willy's face. "A problem?" he said. "How could there be a problem? Find your friend, teach Willy to play the whistle. Doesn't get any simpler than that."

"Right," said Jack.

"So what's the problem?" asked Willy.

"Well, the whistle . . ." Jack didn't know how to finish.

"I'll answer that question," said Annie. "Willy, I'm going to be simple and direct and honest with you."

"Yes . . . ?" said the leprechaun.

"Merlin the magician gave us the whistle to help us on our missions," said Annie. "The whistle is magic, and the magic only works once. Without the magic, I don't really know how to play. So I can't teach you. There you have it."

"Ah," said Willy. He looked at the floor and shook his head. "Then I'm afraid I'm going to have to turn you both into chipmunks."

"*What?*" said Jack.

Willy burst out laughing. "Joking! Only joking!" he said. "Merlin! You should have told me you were friends with Merlin in the first place!"

"Do you know Merlin?" asked Jack.

"Oh, yes, we spent a great deal of time together. Must be about eight hundred years ago now," said Willy. "How is he?"

"He's happy," said Annie.

"Good!" Willy turned back to Mary and Augusta. "I first met the master magician on the Isle of Merlin in the Irish Sea. He—"

"Wait, wait, please, Willy," said Augusta. "Mary, do you have pen and paper?"

"No, my dear, I'm afraid I don't," said Mary.

"I can help," said Jack. He took his pencil and small notebook out of his pocket. He tore some clean pages out of the notebook. Then he gave the pencil and pages to Augusta. "There," he said.

"Oh, thank you, Jack!" said Augusta. She turned back to Willy. "Continue, please."

"Well," said Willy, "Merlin was only a few

centuries old then, and I was a mere lad. . . ."

As Willy told his story, Augusta began to write. Jack put his notebook back into his pocket and nodded to Annie. She nodded back, and the two of them started toward the door.

Just as they were about to leave, Annie called out to the others, "Bye!"

"We have to go home now," said Jack.

"Trip lightly!" said Willy.

"Thank you for everything!" said Augusta.

"One and twenty fare-thee-wells!" said Mary.

"Same to you guys," said Jack. Then he and Annie slipped out of the cottage.

The rain was pouring again, and the wind was blowing hard.

"I think we inspired Augusta," said Annie.

"Yep, we accomplished our mission," said Jack. "Now let's get out of here." He couldn't wait to go home and get warm and dry.

Jack and Annie ran against the wind. They climbed over the stone wall, then hurried down the lane, slipping and sliding in the muck. They ran across the soaked field. By the time they arrived at the rope ladder, their clothes were caked with mud.

Jack and Annie climbed into the tree house. Annie found the Pennsylvania book in the corner. As rain blew through the window, she pointed to a picture of the Frog Creek woods. "I wish we could go there!" she said.

The wind blew harder.

The tree house started to spin.

It spun faster and faster.

Then everything was still.

Absolutely still.

CHAPTER ELEVEN

Lady Gregory

"Ahh, sunshine," said Jack. He closed his eyes and felt the sunshine streaming through the tree house window.

"And clean, dry clothes," murmured Annie. She placed the Pennsylvania book back in the corner.

Jack took the magic whistle out of his pocket and placed it next to the book. "There. Let's go home now," he said. "I want to look on the Internet for information about Augusta." He started down the rope ladder.

"Great idea," said Annie, following Jack. "We

can find out what happened to her."

Jack and Annie ran through the chilly Frog Creek woods. They crossed the street and hurried up the sparkling sidewalk to their yard. They tramped over old snow up to their porch. Annie opened the front door and led the way inside.

"Hi!" Jack called. "We're back!"

"Hi!" their mom called from the kitchen. "Did you have a nice break?"

"Yes, we did!" said Annie.

"Good. Get back to your homework now," said their mom. "So you can finish in time to go to the theater."

"Okay!" called Annie. She went to the computer desk and sat down. "What should I type?" she asked Jack.

Jack pulled up a chair and sat beside her. "Well, we don't know her last name," he said. "So try *Galway . . . Augusta . . .* and *Irish stories.*"

Annie typed these words on the keyboard, then hit *enter.* There were lots of choices for different

Web sites. Annie clicked on the first one.

On the screen was a black-and-white photograph of a woman. The caption under it said:

Lady Augusta Gregory

"Look! It's *her*!" said Annie.

The woman on the screen was middle-aged, but she still looked like Augusta. Her hair was parted neatly down the middle.

Jack read aloud from the screen:

Lady Augusta Gregory was born into a wealthy family in Galway, Ireland, in 1852. She wrote over forty plays and many poems and essays. She was a co-founder of the Abbey Theatre, the national theater of Ireland. Lady Gregory also learned the old language of Ireland and became well known for collecting Irish stories and legends and sharing them with the world.

"Wow!" said Annie. "Augusta *did* have a brave heart and a fine mind! And she must have liked

our play, since she wrote forty of her own and started her own theater."

"Yeah," said Jack. "She really turned out great." This reminded him of a question he'd asked himself earlier. "I wonder what I'm good for? I didn't know how to do anything on that Irish farm."

"Me neither," said Annie. "But hardly any kids today know how to do that kind of stuff."

"So what would we do if all our machines and computers broke down?" said Jack.

"We'd have to figure out how to grow potatoes and make our own clothes and milk cows," said Annie.

"I'd probably read some kind of instructions first, then give it a try," said Jack.

"I'd probably give it a try first," said Annie, "*then* read the instructions."

Jack laughed.

"I know some stuff we're good for," said Annie.

"What?" said Jack.

"First, we're good for helping each other," said Annie.

"Yeah, but—" said Jack.

"No, really. We help each other all the time," said Annie.

"That's true," said Jack.

"*And* we're good for helping Augusta," said

Annie, "and helping Louis Armstrong, Mozart, and Leonardo da Vinci. We put the smile on the Mona Lisa's face, remember?"

Jack nodded. "Yep," he said.

"And we're good for saving an orphan penguin, a huge octopus, and the cities of Tokyo, Venice, and New York," said Annie. "We're good for rescuing a baby gorilla from a leopard, and schoolkids from a twister. We're good for helping Shakespeare, Clara Barton, and George Washington. We're good for rescuing two kids from a tsunami, a Lakota boy from a buffalo stampede, and a baby kangaroo and a koala from a forest fire. We're good for—"

"Wait, stop," said Jack. "Stop."

"But that's not even half of it," said Annie.

"I know," said Jack. "But that's plenty. I'm inspired. I'm ready to write that story for homework. I'll use my own experience. I have a little more than I thought."

"Cool," said Annie. She went back to reading about Lady Gregory on the computer.

Jack grabbed a pencil and pulled out his note-book. He moved to the couch and sat down. As late-winter light slanted into the living room, he began to write.

More Facts from Jack and Annie

Irish Fairies

• There was a time when many people in Ireland believed in fairies who lived inside mounds of earth. The name for Irish fairies is *Sí*. In Ireland, the word *Sí* is pronounced *Shee*. To avoid confusion in my story, I refer to the fairies as the Shee.

• Leprechauns are a type of male Irish fairy. In folktales they often work as shoemakers or tailors and are thought to have hidden pots of gold. Leprechauns are featured on St. Patrick's Day, a national holiday in Ireland celebrated on March 17.

Lady Gregory

• When she was a child, Lady Gregory's full name was Isabella Augusta Persse, though everyone called her Augusta. After she grew up, she married Sir William Henry Gregory. As the wife of a knight, she was called Lady Gregory.

• Ireland's most famous poet is William Butler Yeats (YATES). He was a very good friend of Lady Gregory's. Together in 1904, they founded Dublin's Abbey Theatre, the national theater of Ireland.

• William Butler Yeats often accompanied Lady Gregory when she visited cottages and collected Irish folklore. It was said that Lady Gregory had a natural genius for remembering the direct speech of storytellers. "In her many years of traveling, listening, transcribing and publishing, Lady Gregory . . . gave value to the stories, to the mind and the imagination of Irish country people" (Lucy McDiarmid and Maureen Waters, introduction to *Lady Gregory: Selected Writings*).

Irish Language

• From the 1600s to the early 1900s, the language of Ireland, called *Irish Gaelic*, was replaced by English in many parts of Ireland. During the struggle for Irish independence in the twentieth century, the desire to learn the old language became very strong in Ireland. In 1922, Irish Gaelic became the official language of the country along with English. Today it is taught in Irish public schools. Lady Gregory's knowledge of Irish Gaelic helped her when she visited cottages and collected stories.

Want to learn more about leprechauns and Irish folklore?

Get the facts behind the fiction in the Magic Tree House® Research Guide.

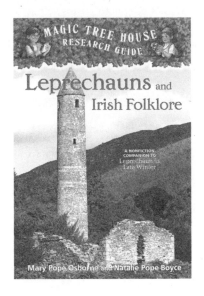

Available now!

Coming September 2010

Don't miss Magic Tree House® #44
(A Merlin Mission)

A Ghost Tale
for Christmas Time

Jack and Annie must bring ghosts
to life to inspire Charles Dickens
to write a masterpiece.